No Exit For U

Matson Sinclair

Published by Crackling Prose Publishing, 2022.

NO EXIT FOR U

First edition. November 10, 2022.

Copyright © 2022 Matson Sinclair.

ISBN: 979-8215221785

Written by Matson Sinclair.

Chapter 1

Dwight spat through his open truck window as I approached. The impact of saliva raised a puff of white dust before beginning to soak into the limestone gravel. I nodded as I passed and he slid out of his truck to follow me up the steps into Holsteins, the neighborhood bar and gathering place. Bill Belmont sat in one of the wooden chairs arrayed on the surrounding veranda sipping on a Coors tall boy, and rose as we reached the top.

"Half a dozen God-damn skeletons costing me almost a hundred thousand dollars in lost land sales," Dwight said as we stomped our feet at the top – a habit drilled into dusty country children at an early age, a nod to the futile attempt to keep the limestone powder at bay. As we entered I raised a finger as a casual wave at Candy behind the bar, where she held court with the early evening regulars, and the three of us passed through the door into the cavernous back room. It had been home to every social event in town as long as anyone alive could remember, but tonight was the semi-weekly town council meeting.

Presiding, as always, was mayor Coup. Coup being his surname as well as the name of the town. His great grandfather had founded the town, really at the time just his employees, and the family had been supplying mayors ever since. Today, among most present anyway, he was simply called Coup.

Also present was Ernesto Sanchez, who owned several thousand acres to the south of town. A thoughtful man, he was believed to have connections to the state government, although there was no concrete proof of this. He employed a cadre of Hispanic farm hands, each carefully monitored for valid green card status.

Today's special guests were setting up an easel with a series of large printed sheets attached at the top. Representatives of the state highway planning commission, they were scheduled to bring us up to date regarding plans for the long-awaited interstate highway passing just to the east of town. Five chairs were arranged in an arc facing the easel, with Mayor Coup taking the farthest left, Ernesto at his right. I sat in the center and Dwight sat to my right. Bill had settled into a captain's chair behind us just inside the door, tilted back against the wall as usual.

"Hello, gentlemen," said the taller, younger and darker haired of our visitors. "Thank you for letting us speak with you this evening." Motioning to Bill, "Would you care to join us up here, sir?"

Bill shook his head, and Coup answered, "No, he's technically a spectator. We are still short one council member. He should be along any minute."

The state man nodded, and stood by the easel. His cohort, grey haired and carrying the beginning of a paunch, pulled up a chair to his side.

Bill drained the last of his Coors, and with a practiced motion reached behind himself and opened the door, placing the empty just inside the jamb in the bar area, where Candy would be watching for it. As he was reaching to close the door, Harold Simmons, the newest member of the council rushed in wearing a grey sports coat and a tie. "Thanks, Bill," he said as he stepped through, as if Bill had opened the door for him.

Harold sat, and Coup said "The meeting of the town council will come to order." Rather a humorous statement as he had never stated it before, and there was no secretary to record any of the proceedings. Out of respect for Coup I did not crack a smile, nor did anyone else I could see, although I couldn't now see Bill as I had turned to the man with the easel. "These gentlemen from the state have offered to fill us in on the latest plans for the new interstate construction".

"Thank you, Mr. Mayor," stated the taller man. "My name is Montgomery Rellette, and this is Mr. Gerald Thomas. We are with the State Planning Board and wish to present the revised plan for construction of the extension for the interstate making the final link to the existing transverse interstate highways." He peeled back the top cover sheet and we all looked at the map. I could see where the revised path of the interstate would cross substantially less land owned by Dwight and more land owned by Coup and myself. I could hear the sound of the door behind us opening, and the sound of a new tall boy being delivered and opened for Bill.

Rellette used a laser pointer to trace the new highway in red from the top to the bottom. "As the new highway moves south from Williams County it enters Barnstable County where an exit will connect with the existing US highway continuing south to Barnstable town. The new interstate then loops west into Silver County to avoid the existing Signal Hill Wildlife Refuge and begins a gentle turn back to the east and into Barnstable County where a new bridge for County Route U will incorporate an exit for Coup town before continuing..."

"Don't want no exit," came the voice from behind us. Rellette stopped. We all turned to look at Bill.

"No exit?" repeated Harold with incredulity.

We all looked at each other, a certain level of dumbfoundedness passing around the room. Dwight scratched his ear, a sure sign of deep thought. Coup looked down at his folded hands and said, "Let's allow Mr. Rellette to finish his presentation."

Rellette returned his pointer to the map. "The revision of the planned route passing closer to Coup town than originally intended is due to the recent designation of the USGS Center for Antiquities Study Area situated between the east and west units of the Signal Hill Wildlife Refuge. This creates a barrier which must be passed either to the east or west. To the east, urban sprawl from Barnstable town adjacent the Wildlife Refuge would require extensive cost and upheaval of residences and industry, while there is ample space to the west of the Wildlife Refuge currently utilized for crops and livestock. No relocation of any existing structures or families would be necessary."

"After passing the western edge of the Wildlife Refuge and proceeding south under a new County Route U bridge – with or without an exit - the new highway continues south southeast where another exit will connect to the existing US highway proceeding south from Barnstable town."

"So Barnstable gets 3 exits," commented Dwight.

"Well," said Rellette, "Yes." He pointed to the northern most exit for the US Highway. "There is one," he moved the pointer down to Highway U. "There is the second which accesses County Route U connecting both to Coup town to the west and Barnstable town to the east." He moved the pointer down to the southern exit, "And here is the third where an exit accesses the US Highway south of Barnstable town."

"But let me point out," he raised the pointer back to the route U bridge. "The state has no plan to pave County Route U the 3 miles into Barnstable town. We would only supply pavement to the end of the access ramp. It is, after all, a county road, and east of the new interstate it lies entirely within Barnstable County."

"So, you wouldn't pave Route U into Coup either?" asked Ernesto.

"Technically, no, since U is a County Road not a State Highway, although the distance from the top of the exit ramp where our pavement ends to the Coup city limit is less than a thousand feet."

"Don't want no exit" repeated Bill.

Harold turned and asked "Why wouldn't you want an exit?"

"Brings the outside world in. Full of drugs, thieves, trouble." He paused for a drink. "We got us a real nice little town here; don't want to mess that up." He nodded, agreeing with himself.

"Mr. Rellette," said Coup. "Would we have the option of declining an exit to be constructed for Route U?"

Rellette looked at his partner, Thomas, who had not said a word. "Well," said Thomas, "Since it would technically save the state money, that could possibly be an option."

Harold looked at the other town council members. "You can't seriously be considering not having an exit," he pleaded. "Here is the opportunity this community needs – we have no growth, no industry, just a fading past. We're lucky the town hasn't dried up and blown away."

Coup pawed at the air with his right hand. "We'll discuss this idea at length Harold. I understand exactly what you're saying, and while I tend to agree with you I am not sure everyone in the community would share your view." Turning to Rellette, "Mr. Rellette, pardon the interruption. Do you have anything else to add?"

Rellette shook his head and turned to Thomas for agreement. When Thomas nodded, Rellette said "No, that about sums it up. We will be contacting the individual land owners soon to discuss acreage and purchase details, as well as access to separated parcels."

"Separated parcels?" I asked.

"Well, yes," Rellette replied as I heard another tall boy opening behind me. "Some parcels of land will be bisected by the highway, leaving orphaned partial parcels without access for the existing land owner."

"So you put the highway through the middle of a field, and now I can't get to my land on the other side," I said.

"Exactly," said Rellette. "There are a number of remediations possible including land sales to adjacent owners, access creation, or possibly sale to the state. These will be discussed with the owners on a parcel by parcel basis."

"Thank you, gentlemen," said Coup. "I suggest we adjourn for a brief recess while our guests gather their equipment and resume in a few minutes."

Dwight and I headed out into the bar area, and Harold trotted along behind. "Can you believe it?" he asked with incredulity. "No exit!" He shook his head.

The bar business had picked up a little, three tables were occupied, and two of these groups were munching on burgers, the third occupied by locals sharing a pitcher. We walked up to the right hand side of the bar and Candy met us. "What'll it be fellas?" she smiled.

"Miller Lite," said Harold.

Dwight just looked at me. This was a complication I had created by suggesting Bill step down from the council due to his excessive alcohol consumption, having been replaced by Harold. The key word there, we all knew, was excessive. We were all adults here, and all agreed there was nothing wrong with having a beer, but to dip into the same territory which had let to Bill's ouster was a touchy subject. The fact that Harold was oblivious to all this only added to the problem.

"I'll have a Coke" I said looking back at Dwight.

"Me too," he replied, meeting my gaze.

"Ice?" Candy asked. We both shook our heads. Candy set two cans of Coke on the bar and opened each one, and poured a Miller Lite for Harold. We watched wordlessly, until she finished and went to check on other customers. "No exit!" repeated Harold, still shaking his head.

We took our drinks and returned to the back room where the state boys had vacated. Ernesto had rearranged the chairs (excepting Bills, still back against the doorframe) into a circle.

Less formally now Coup began "The idea of foregoing an exit is an interesting one. I can see many different sides to the issue."

Harold was shaking his head again in disgust "How can we even think of turning down an opportunity like this! It's the first real chance at success this town has seen in years!"

"Perhaps we should have a straw poll to see how we are leaning" suggested Coup, always at the helm. "Those in favor of an exit –..."

Harold and I each raised our right hand. Dwight just looked at me.

"Those opposed -..." Ernesto and Dwight each raised their right hand.

"It would seem we are divided in our opinions," mused Coup. "Rather than casting a deciding vote, since this is just a straw poll, I suggest we table the issue for discussion until our next meeting." There were nods around the circle, except of course for Harold who continued to shake his head in exasperation.

"A lot of folks might like to weigh in on this," I said. "Maybe I can talk to some of the townsfolk and get a feel for how they think."

"Good idea, Sam," replied the Mayor. "We're adjourned."

If he'd had a gavel he would have banged it, providing he also had something to bang it on.

Chapter 2

"No exit for U?" asked Suzie as I stepped through the back door.

I had long ago stopped being stunned by the speed of the gossip network in the small town. Of course, Suzie, being the town's only hairdresser had her finger on the pulse more than anyone.

"Well, I voted for it."

"Oh, you already had a vote?" Suzie tapped the spoon on the side of the pan and turned, giving me a peck on the cheek.

"Not really. Just a straw poll." I pulled a bottle of beer from the fridge and sat at the kitchen table.

"So it was Ernesto, Dwight and Bill holding out?" She pulled 2 plates from the cupboard.

"What are you drinking?" I asked.

"Milk," she replied.

I arose and retrieved a glass and the milk, pouring her a generous portion. "Bill doesn't get a vote." I placed the milk at her spot as she dished up 2 plates of pasta.

"So, what's the plan now?" Suzie asked.

"Check the pulse of the town."

Suzie grinned the grin I had fallen in love with. "So, you need my help."

Later that evening we sat together in the swing behind the house. It had originally been suspended from the front porch, but we had moved it to the backyard where I had built a frame. We could now lean back and look deep into the night sky, the stars swaying as we gently swung together.

Suzie curled up close as the May evening air cooled, her head on my shoulder, my arm wrapped around her. We were quiet, a comfortable silence, as was often the case. We had covered the topics needing discussion at dinner, catching each other up on the day's events.

Eventually she asked "How close will the new road be to our house?"

I pointed east. "It will be just below the pasture behind Marjorie's place, heading deeper into the valley as it goes south."

"So, it will be out of sight?" Suzie looked up at me with her big brown eyes.

"Yes, I think so."

We were both quiet for a time. I contemplated the grasshoppers munching in the grass, legs rubbing together in their telltale sound.

"But not for Marjorie," said Suzie.

"What's that?" I asked.

"It won't be out of sight for Marjorie."

"Oh, no," I agreed. "She will be able to see it from anywhere on that side of her house."

"And people on the road will see her," Suzie mused. "She'll have no privacy at all."

We sat in silence for a while. Suzie snuggled closer. I held her tight. "You want me to get you a sweater?" I asked.

"No," she sighed. "I like it just like this."

I thought for a while. "Marjorie could build a fence," I suggested.

I felt Suzie nod against my chest.

"Will we be able to hear it?" Suzie looked up at me again. "I mean, hear traffic on the highway?"

"I suppose so." I said.

"But that will be the case whether there's an exit or not," she said after a while.

"What's that?"

"Sound from the highway." Suzie looked up at me. "We'll hear the sound from the highway whether there is an exit or not."

"True," I nodded in agreement.

"Would there be a gas station at the exit?" she asked.

"That would be up to whoever wanted to build one," I replied. "But I suppose there would. Most exits have a station."

"And maybe a fast food restaurant too."

"Yes," I nodded.

"Those could make jobs for local people," she said. "Right now there are so few jobs to be had in town."

"Harold's point exactly."

"Would people take this exit to get to Silver Lake?" she asked.

I thought about this. Silver Lake was the county seat 11 miles to the west on gravel Route U. Currently, most people accessed that town by the paved state highway running north and south, unless they were starting out in Coup.

"Most people aren't going to want to drive the 11 miles of gravel to Silver Lake" I replied. "So I think the answer is 'No.'"

Suzie snuggled closer and tightened her grip around my waist. I squeezed her shoulder as we swayed beneath the starry sky.

Chapter 3

"I thought it was supposed to go down through the valley," said Marjorie gruffly.

"It was," I agreed. "But they changed it."

"Because of some Indian bones?" she asked.

"There was a story about it in the paper."

"I know," she nodded. "I read it. Some damn kids found bones up at Indian Bend Campground and they took 'em to the anthropology lab at the university. Carbon dated to be some of the oldest found in the country. Sent a team to start excavations." She looked up at me, "You know I used to be a science teacher."

"Yes, I remember." I chuckled. "I was one of your students."

"And a damn poor one," she stomped her cane and turned back toward the valley sloping away from us. "You were always busy making eyes at that little Ramsey girl."

"You know I married her."

"Yes, dammit." She turned back to regard me with distain. "I was at your wedding."

"I didn't know if you remembered."

"I remember everything," she growled. "Right now I'm remembering my sister keeps asking me to move in with her in Boca Raton."

We stood there gazing into the distance where soon 4 lanes of pavement would be carrying the commerce of the country past at 70 miles per hour.

I had begun the morning after breakfast with my daily pasture patrol for inspection of the cattle and water situations. The stock tanks were full, the cattle grazing on new leaves of grass poking up rather than the bales of straw leftover from winter. Seeing all was well, I had started my canvas of the neighborhood by calling on Marjorie, arguably the most affected by the rerouting of the interstate closer to town.

"Bah," she said at length and tromped up the steps into her home, a two-story white frame house dating back to the 1800s. She made no invitation and offered no good-bye.

I left.

I cruised down Main Street, technically State Route U, to Suzie's. A 2-chair beauty salon 1 block south of Holsteins, Suzie ran it by herself, mostly. At various times she had taken in another hairdresser, but they had usually moved on to greener pastures with more clientele. Currently she had one girl, Chloe, who came in on Saturdays to do haircuts, with an emphasis on men's haircuts.

With today being Wednesday, Suzie had both chairs filled as well as one of the driers. She often worked both chairs simultaneously cutting in one while a color was dwelling in the other. I walked in and eyed the pastries and coffee in the waiting area.

"Coffee only for you," Suzie jided. "Croissants are for the paying customers."

I snagged a sweet roll and took a big bite. "Hey," she said, coming over to give me a big push. I grabbed her around the waist and gave her a big frosting laced kiss.

"Get a room!" howled the lady in the nearest chair to laughter and snickers from the room. I released Suzie who returned to cutting hair.

"It's a Danish, not a croissant," said a mouth full of pastry.

"You have frosting on your face," noted Mildred Taylor, seated in the waiting area thumbing thru a 3-month-old magazine.

"He'll be back to get it in a minute," chimed in Aletha Cromwell, her hair in little paper twists in the far chair. Suzie leaned toward the mirror over the sink and brushed off frosting as I poured a cup of Joe.

"Shouldn't you be out building that new freeway?" asked Mildred.

"That's for the young bucks," I said with a slurp.

"He's a councilman," chimed in the lady in the near chair. I looked at her, and knew she was familiar, but I couldn't place her. "Councilmen don't get their hands dirty." More laughter and snickers.

"Tough room," I said, and took another bite.

"He's supposed to be polling the town finding out whether people want an exit for Highway U," said Suzie.

"Maybe that's why he's here," said Aletha.

"No, he's just here to scarf down some sweet rolls." said Mildred.

"And to grab Suzie's sweet rolls," said the lady I couldn't place. Laughter rolled around the room while Suzie looked at me in mock disapproval.

"See what you caused?" she said accusingly.

"Relax honey," I said. "You don't have any rolls other than these pastries."

"If you want to ask about the exit, you should talk to my husband," said the lady in the near chair. Who was she?

"If we don't have an exit, what would we have?" asked Aletha.

"Just a bridge over the highway?" asked Mildred.

"Yes," I replied. "Route U would just have a bridge over the highway."

"That seems a waste to me," said Aletha. "I mean, the highway will be right there, why not have an exit?"

"It would be a lot more convenient," said the lady in the nearest chair.

"It would also be convenient for anyone wanting to cause trouble," stated Mildred matter of factly.

"An exit would almost certainly lead to development in the town," I said.

"Is that a good thing or a bad thing?" asked Mildred.

"Both," said the lady in the chair, Suzie's scissors sending snippets of her hair flying.

"Hold still, Mary," said Suzie helpfully, giving me a wink. Mary, Mary, Mary I thought. Who is she?

"I would like to get a Starbucks," said Aletha.

"A Starbucks!" exclaimed Mary. Turning to me, "Would we be getting a Starbucks?"

"Mary, hold still," said Suzie with the scissors.

"No telling what we might get," I replied.

"Maybe a bar or a strip club," said Mildred. Horrified gasps circled the room.

I waved my hand palm downward in a calming motion. "We can legislate to ban things like a strip club. And a bar would have to apply for a liquor license."

Mary said "Holsteins is a bar."

Quiet descended in the room, save for the snipping above Mary's neck and the soft purr of the hairdryer.

Suzy pointed with her scissors. "Mary had a good idea. Why don't you go over and talk with Mr. Palmetter?"

Palmetter! That was it! Mary Palmetter! Finally, my memory produced the link. I had never seen one without the other. Mary and Harry Palmetter.

I refilled my coffee and bid the ladies adieu. I climbed into my truck for the short drive to Palmetter's house at the west edge of town. It was a sprawling brick and stone ranch house surrounded on both sides by a high evergreen hedge. The driveway along the east side of the house ended at a wooden gate.

I parked the truck and walked up to the door and knocked. A few seconds later, the gate at the end of the driveway opened, and out stepped Harry Palmetter. "Thought I heard a car," he said walking toward me, extending his hand. I shook it.

"Good morning, Mr. Palmetter," I offered.

"That it is, that it is," he turned and walked back toward the gate. "Come along Sam, but call me Harry."

I followed him through the gate, which he shut behind us, into the back yard. I stood in amazement. The evergreen hedge alongside the house made a right angle turn and extended into the distance on both sides. Stretching into the distance was also a strip of asphalt, widening at midpoint, and ending in the distance with a circle turn around.

Idling near us outside an open garage was a beautiful light blue low-slung car. My brain, overloaded, searched for a make and model. "Imperial?" I asked.

"Correct," nodded Harry. "Not *Chrysler* Imperial, this was built when they had dropped the Chrysler name and were calling it a separate make, just 'Imperial'".

I walked around the car, taking in its proportions. It was big, very big, and wide, but it carried all its bulk down low. At the rear, large chrome and glass light assemblies sat atop sizeable, but not overwhelming fins. The interior was a combination of blue and white, chrome glistening on many surfaces. The entire car looked like it had just rolled off a showroom floor. "What year?" I asked.

"Nineteen sixty-two," replied Harry, patting the roof. "This was the first year they started to tone down the fins, but they kept the gunsight taillights."

"Where did you get it?" I asked, still circling the car.

"Well, I used to run a body shop between here and Memphis," he began. "One day some kid is getting his Chevy repaired after running it into a ditch, and mentions his grandpa had an old car in his barn." Harry shook his head. "Didn't even know what kind. Only knew it was blue." He opened the driver's door and motioned for me to get in. I did, sinking into the upholstery while the heavy V8 engine rumbled. "I went to see his grandpa, who said it was a 62 Imperial Crown Southampton. I asked to see it, and he said he wasn't interested in selling it unless it was to someone who would keep it and take care of it. He didn't want it hot rodded or used in a demolition derby."

Harry watched as I blipped the throttle, the torque rocking the big coupe. "They eventually outlawed these at the demolition derbies, they were too strong and overwhelmed other cars. So, he let me look at it, but I tell ya, his idea of taking care of a car was pretty different from mine. It was filthy dirty and hadn't been run in years. I had to rebuild the engine and brakes, remove and refurbish the gas tank, all kinds of things. But she cleaned up pretty nice, eh?"

"It's beautiful," I agreed.

"Want to go for a ride?" he asked.

"Uh, sure," I said. "I'll just move my truck" as I climbed out.

"Oh, ho, ho," laughed Harry, sliding behind the wheel and motioning me toward the passenger side. "Not out there, *here*!" and he pointed to the asphalt strip running behind the house."

I seated myself, closed the door, and Harry pushed a button on the dash. The transmission slipped into gear and we glided forward down the asphalt strip, slowly gathering speed. Along the right-hand side was a row of sheds with garage doors, all closed but one.

"This is what I do every day," said Harry. "Cars don't like to sit, they need to be driven. So, I drive one of 'em every day unless it's raining."

"One of them?" I asked.

"Ha, ha," he laughed. "Well, I've been collecting for quite a while. Ended up with ones I really like." We were approaching the far end of the asphalt and he slowed some for the turn around, which I now saw was slightly banked. He pressed the accelerator as we exited the turn and we rocketed down the lane toward the house. At the wide spot, halfway along I realized there was a sizeable hump built into one side of the road. "Hang on!" said Harry as we hit the hump at 30 miles per hour. The car seemed to lift into the air then settled with a bounce as Harry touched the brake.

"What?" I asked in amazement.

"Gotta exercise the whole car, and I have limited space. That includes exercising the suspension. The torsion bars and shocks will start to deteriorate if you don't run them through their entire travel." He had turned at the house and we began a second lap.

"How many cars do you have?" I asked.

"Six, but that includes my pickup and Mary's Toyota," he said, steering clear of the hump. "That's why my ears perked up when I heard there may or may not be an exit for the new highway."

"So, you would prefer an exit?" I asked.

"Hell yes!" exclaimed Harry. "I can't take these classics out on a dusty gravel road! Gotta have concrete or asphalt. I've spent too much time and effort on every nut and bolt in these things to let them get all caked with dirt and dust." He had swung around the far turn in the other direction, making a right turn instead of a left at the circle. We sped back toward the house, thankfully skipping the hump this time. The car felt smooth and powerful.

"Even if we get an exit, only the bridge itself will be concrete, extending to where the entrance and exit ramps intersect. The short distance to the town and the city streets would still be gravel," I pointed out.

Harry slowed and stopped the car outside the garage, pressing a button on the dash to take it out of gear. He turned to me, "Surely the city could pave the road from the exit to the town, and I bet people would like to have at least main street paved as well."

I got out of the car, as did Harry. "Harry," I said. "We have no city tax. We have no income or cash reserves to pay for any road improvements." I shook my head and held my hands out palms up. "That would be the county's decision whether to pave the road, not the city."

"Silver County," said Harry.

"Yes," I replied. "The highway itself will be just over the line in Barnstable county but Route U from the highway to here would be in Silver county."

"I bet some of the townspeople would kick in to pave that little section from the ramp into town, and Main street too" said Harry.

"Maybe," I said doubtfully, looking at the beautiful blue car idling in the late morning sun.

Chapter 4

"Hello, Muskrats!" exclaimed Dwight as he reached for the screen door, the open front door providing all the invitation country folk required. 'Muskrats' being the name he had called the two of us since America's 1973 cover of *Muskrat Love*.

We were expecting him. He and Suzie had spoken earlier in the week, Dwight proposing to take us for ice cream if we would feed him dinner.

"What are you drinking, Dwight?" Suzie came out of the kitchen to give Dwight a big hug and a peck on the cheek. "And where's Homer?"

"Homer doesn't leave home these days," Dwight shook his head. "Too hard for him to climb in and out of the truck."

"Oh," Suzie sighed. "That's so sad. But I'll pack him a doggie bag for later." As she turned to head back into the kitchen she said over her shoulder, "So what are you drinking?"

"What are we having?" asked Dwight, turning to hang his well-seasoned straw cowboy hat on the rack inside the doorway.

"Roast with potatoes and carrots, gravy, hot rolls and butter," Suzie replied.

"Sounds like a beer to me," said Dwight.

"Me too!" I added.

"Great!" exclaimed Suzie. "Sam, get 2 beers and pour me a glass of Riesling."

I stood and headed for the kitchen. Dwight winked and followed me.

Dwight took a deep inhale of the aromas and said "Sure smells good."

"That kinda talk will get you seconds," said Suzie.

"My plan," replied Dwight, giving me another wink as I reached inside the refrigerator.

In the end, we all had seconds, even Suzie who normally was restrained in her appetite. I refilled her wine and grabbed a second beer, but Dwight declined. Talk ranged from crops to cattle, kids and grandkids, but without mention of the upcoming construction.

When Suzie had finished her wine, we all got up and quickly cleared the table, me rinsing the dishes and Dwight loading the dishwasher. Suzie transferred the leftovers to appropriate storage containers, including a generous portion for Homer, and stowed them in the fridge.

As I wiped my hands on the dishtowel, Dwight asked "Are we ready?"

Suzie and I said 'yes' and grabbed jackets as we walked out the door, Dwight retrieving his hat. As we stepped out front, it was obvious Dwight's dusty old pickup was not going to be our ride. Out front was a new-ish four door pickup truck.

I looked at Dwight and raised an eyebrow.

"Daughter's truck," he said. "Can't have Suzie riding around in a dusty old pickup like mine."

"Thank you, Dwight," said Suzie slipping her arm around Dwight's elbow. "You know I grew up riding in dusty old pickups."

"Yeah," he said. "But times, they are a-changing."

We clambered into the truck, Dwight driving and Suzie riding shotgun. I relaxed in back behind her. He drove up to Main St., then turned right heading east towards Barnstable. We cruised slowly, down the slope into the valley where soon 4 lanes of traffic would be traveling, and continued across the low-water bridge over Silver Creek.

The bridge was simple in design, a series of culverts with fill and a paved section of roadway just above. At high water, which only followed local heavy rains, the creek would rise above the roadway, and the road would be closed until the level returned to normal, and the County Engineer (Barnstable County at this point) would inspect the bridge and declare it safe for traffic.

We continued on the road, now gravel again, into Barnstable, and Dwight turned left, to the north on the paved US Highway.

"Isn't the ice cream shop to the right? "asked Suzie, knowing full well it was.

"Different ice cream place", replied Dwight, with a twinkle in his eye. Now that we were on the pavement he picked up speed as we rolled out of town. We cruised through the countryside with the sky darkening as the sun set to our left. We continued into Williams county and proceeded north. I knew Dwight was up to something, but had no clue what. I was sure Suzie was likewise in the dark.

Eventually we came to the outskirts of Forest City. Soon a place called Fritz's Custard appeared on our left. A smattering of cars was in the parking lot, some with ice-cream eating people inside, their windows rolled down. Other people were seated on tables outside.

Dwight pulled in and parked. We got out, and walked toward the establishment. The extensive menu was above a row of windows, each with a short line, where employees took orders and delivered ice cream.

We each placed an order, and Dwight paid. As the ice cream was delivered, Suzie took hers and walked toward an empty table.

"Hold on," called Dwight. "Let's take a short ride."

We resumed our places in the truck and Dwight drove westward down a country lane. Soon we came to an overpass crossing the existing Interstate Highway, passing below us at an oblique angle as it swung north to bypass Forest City.

"I'm resetting the trip meter," said Dwight, then continued westward. Eying the odometer, he drove slowly, then turned left into a short driveway leading to a pasture. "Okay," he said. "We're 6 tenths of a mile past the Interstate." He pointed, "It's actually a little closer than that because we didn't cross it at a right angle, but this will give us an idea."

"An idea of what?" asked Suzie.

"Of what it will be like to live 6 tenths of a mile from the interstate," explained Dwight, as he got out of the truck.

We followed as he lowered the tailgate of the truck. We placed our ice creams dishes on the tailgate so I could boost Suzie into the bed, where she sat on the side and reached for her ice cream. Dwight and I each sat on the tailgate and ate.

We ate slowly, the evening sounds of the country glade being in the forefront. Crickets, the wind in the trees, the occasional distant sound of a dog barking (or his non-domesticated cousin).

There was also a distant hum of traffic. Not a roar, more of a quiet low whistle. I thought it was mostly the tires on pavement we were hearing, with a little wind disturbance and engine noise thrown in. Constant, but varying in intensity. We sat there quietly and ate and listened. The sun having set, and there being no moon, the sky was filled with stars, the Milky Way plainly visible.

"It's not that bad," opined Suzie quietly.

I agreed.

We sat there some time, the ice cream long gone. The night air settled around us, cooling. We were glad we had brought the jackets along.

At length Dwight said, "There's something else I need to show you."

I helped Suzie down and we packed our trash in a bag provided by Dwight. We reloaded and headed back into town. At the state highway Dwight turned north and cruised through town passing various businesses until we neared the entrance ramp for the interstate highway passing on the north side of town. Several gas stations and fast food restaurants lined the state highway at this point. Dwight overshot the interstate then turned left into a burger joint. He drove through the parking lot and made a right turn onto the state highway now headed back south. As he passed beneath the highway he again reset the odometer.

He drove slowly as we passed the various businesses arrayed along the main street clustered south of the exit, then turned onto a side street and drove 2 blocks more. He stopped at a closed muffler shop and we got out. Again we assembled ourselves at the back of the truck with Suzie in the bed and Dwight and myself on the tailgate. Dwight said nothing. We all sat there quietly, listening.

"Are we the same distance away from the highway?" Suzie asked at length.

"Yes," replied Dwight.

"It doesn't seem any louder here," she offered. "If anything, it seems less loud."

"There is less noise from critters," I said. "Maybe more city sounds but less highway noise."

Dwight nodded.

"Is there something else?" asked Suzie. "Something we're not getting?"

Again, Dwight nodded.

The three of us sat there. Quietly listening and looking. I closed my eyes. I heard cars on the street, an occasional stereo. The traffic from the interstate was, as Suzie said, less noticeable than before.

"Oh My God!" Suzie exclaimed at length. I opened my eyes to see her staring up at the sky in alarm. "There's no stars!" She looked at me and at Dwight, not understanding.

"Light pollution," said Dwight.

I looked up at the night sky and saw he was right. There were a few stars, but only the brightest could be seen, maybe a dozen or so. Certainly no Milky Way.

"So, this isn't caused by the interstate?" asked Suzie.

"No, I think its caused by all the lights of the business surrounding the exit. And the street lights." Dwight dipped his head, his eyes in shadow from his hat.

Suzie looked at me and spoke in earnest. "Sam, we can't have an exit. We would lose our starry sky!"

Chapter 5

We were gathered as before in the back of Holstein's. Coup had asked me to share my findings regarding the mood of the townspeople.

"In general, the younger folk favor an exit while the older residents lean towards keeping it as it is," I reported. "There are exceptions, of course. For instance, Harry Palmetter really wants a paved road, but I explained that even if we had an exit there was no money to pave the road into town. And Dwight pointed out that development resulting from an exit would add lighting, and this would cause light pollution resulting in the loss of our night sky."

There was nodding around the room, except for Harold. "Night sky?" he asked. "We would hinder development just to protect our view of the stars?"

Again, there was nodding.

"I wonder," said Ernesto. "Is there a way to make everyone happy?"

"How do you mean?" asked Mayor Coup.

"Well, we have some people who want pavement and better access to the outside world, but we have others who don't want the immediate connection provided by the interstate." Again, there was nodding around the room. Ernesto continued, "Is there a way to improve our access without getting an exit?"

There was silence around the room.

"We have *got* to have an exit," said Harold.

"Pave Highway U," said Bill from his tilted chair inside the doorway.

"How would we do that?" I asked. "There's no money."

"Sure there's money," said Bill. "The county has money; the City of Coup could raise money. Hell, most of us in this room are making serious money from land sales to the state for right of way on the new interstate."

We all pondered this.

"Route U into Barnstable Town is all in Barnstable County from the new interstate into Barnstable Town," remarked Dwight.

"So any improvements in Route U to the east of the interstate would require agreement from Barnstable County," I continued the thought.

"I wonder if Barnstable County would provide part of the funding," added Ernesto.

We all looked at each other.

"Could it be that easy?" asked Ernesto.

"This is an interesting idea," said Mayor Coup. "I suggest we authorize Sam and Dwight to approach the Barnstable County government and measure interest in this proposition." He raised his hand, "All agreed?"

Everyone, even Harold, raised their hand. Bill sipped from his tall boy.

Chapter 6

The next day Dwight picked me up in his daughter's truck. He was wearing clean jeans and a shirt with a bolo tie; I wore a tweed sport coat over a collared shirt. We were stylish members of the local government preparing to call on neighboring politicians to ask for money.

Dwight drove down Route U past the site of the new interstate, past the road to his place and the new Center for Antiquities Study Area, across the low water bridge over Silver Creek, and up the hill towards Barnstable Town. Route U continued as a gravel road until it entered the Barnstable Town city limits, then became paved with blacktop. We continued to the state highway, then turned left the two blocks to the county courthouse.

We parked and went inside to the Barnstable County Commissioner's office. A secretary with salt and pepper hair in a print dress with a white sweater greeted us. We explained who we were and asked to see the Commissioner. From inside the open door behind her came a voice, "Beula, send them on in."

She waved us through and we entered a good-sized office with a large wooden desk behind which a man in a long-sleeved white shirt with tie was rising and extending a hand. He was tall and slim, red of face, with a long thin nose atop which perched black rimmed spectacles. Wisps of greying hair topped his crown.

We each shook his hand, and I introduced us.

"Wilton Greenville," he said. "I'm fairly new to this position, I came on to help manage the growth era Barnstable is entering." We all sat. I noticed several piles of large plans in stacks around the room. "We forecast this new interstate to bring in a lot of new commerce and we're poised to take full advantage of it." Gee, I thought, Harold is in the wrong town...

"So, what can I do for you gentlemen?" he asked.

"Our town is considering some expansion as well," I said. "But we're wanting to hold it in check and make only a small number of changes."

"Yes," he nodded in agreement. "I heard you might even be opting out of having an exit built for Route U."

"That's correct," I replied. "Which is what led us here to your office." Greenville looked questioningly as I continued. "We are thinking it might be more beneficial to both our towns to simply improve Route U between the two towns, Coup and Barnstable. That would give our residents access to the interstate through Barnstable Town without creating the traffic from a new exit for Route U."

"Thereby increasing the traffic in Barnstable Town," he added.

"Yes," I agreed. "The traffic and the commerce".

"But you would submit a full proposal to the Barnstable County Board," said Greenville.

"Of course," I agreed.

"We're just here today to measure the interest in our idea," offered Dwight. "No sense making a full proposal unless we knew it would be looked on kindly."

"Of course," nodded Greenville. "Exactly what I would do." He stood, put his hands in his pockets, and walked toward the window, looking out, as if deep in thought. "You boys in a hurry?" he asked.

"No," we replied in unison, shaking our heads.

Greenville picked up the phone on his desk and hit a single button. In a brief moment he was connected with someone. "Is he in?" he spoke into the handset. After a moment, he replied "I have some gentlemen from the Coup City Council here, could we drop by for a moment?" Again he listened, then added an "Okay," and replaced the phone.

Grabbing a suit coat from the rack by the doorway he said "Let's walk across the street." Dwight and I followed him, with Dwight giving me a knowing look.

We exited the side door of the courthouse and walked across the street to the Barnstable Town City Hall. Greenville led us up the stairs to the second floor where a sign said "The Honorable Randall Barnes, Mayor". We entered the outer office where a young blonde girl with her hair up in a bun waved at him. He led us into the back office where The Honorable Randall Barnes waited.

"Hello Dwight, Sam", he greeted us, not bothering to stand.

Greenville said, in surprise, "Oh, you know these gentlemen?"

"Barney," said Dwight, reaching across the desk for a handshake.

Barnes rose, and took the hand. "These days its Mayor Barnes, if you don't mind Dwight."

I offered my hand, Barnes shook it as well, and I simply said "Mr. Mayor."

We all sat. The room was paneled in a dark wood, with tinted windows overlooking Main St. Barnes's desk was huge and clean. Not a scrap of paper littered it or the office.

Greenville started by repeating in essence what Dwight and I had proposed.

Barnes listened as he relit a cigar and got it going, rotating it as he puffed and leaned back in his chair, his feet propped on a corner of his desk.

"Thing is," he said when Greenville finished. "We have some pretty strict ordinances regarding construction in Barnstable County. Reworking a main artery such as Route U would require it be brought up to code." He brought his feet down and leaned into his desk, elbows down. "Especially the crossing of Silver Creek. That low water bridge has been a hazard for years, and I've had to use my influence to keep it from being closed altogether. A new bridge there alone would be what, Greenville?"

"I don't think it could be done for less than a million, probably closer to a million five," said Greenville.

"So, you're talking about over a million for the bridge, plus reworking what, 2 miles of roadway to code, with ditches, substrate, concrete, signage, guardrails. I would bet you're talking close to two million."

"Closer to 3 miles total," said Dwight.

"There you go," said Barnes. "Well over two million for the project." He puffed on his cigar. "You boys got that kind of money?"

"Since the road itself is in Barnstable County we were hoping Barnstable County would help with the funding," I suggested.

Barnes laughed, a sneering sort of laugh, which eventually made him choke on his cigar smoke. He eventually regained his composure, and shook his head. "Fellas, I gotta admire you. But Barnstable Town and Barnstable County have their hands full with projects to improve access to the state highway in preparation for its connections with the new interstate. We simply don't have the funds to offer charity road projects for our shirt-tail neighbors. I don't even know for sure that we'll be able to keep that low water bridge open over Silver Creek."

He stood and offered his had again as a signal that the meeting was over. "Thank y'all for stopping by. And good luck!"

Greenville led us out. We thanked him for his time and walked to the truck. Once we were inside Dwight started the truck and looked at me.

"The Honorable Randall Barnes," I said.

"Freakin' Barney Fife," replied Dwight. "I knew the second Greenville picked up that phone."

"In hindsight, it was a fool's errand," I said. "But we had to do it."

"What now?" asked Dwight as he headed down Route U towards Coup.

"Plan B," I replied.

"Which is?"

"I dunno. But we gotta think of something."

Chapter 7

"Poor baby," Suzie said, wrapping her arms around my head and pulling it close to her bosom. "Did the scary old Mayor Man make you run away?"

"Mmpf mmpf", I said into her breasts.

She released me and went back to the stove.

"Dwight predicted it," I said. "The whole thing. The new County Commissioner turning to Barney and a flat rejection."

"Well it was a great idea, getting a paved road without an exit. Too bad you couldn't do it in Silver County."

The aroma of pan fried chicken filled the kitchen. "You want to mash the potatoes?" she asked.

I said "Sure," and went to the refrigerator for the milk. I drained the large cubed potatoes Suzie had cooked and placed them one at a time into the ricer, squeezing out perfect lump-less mashed potatoes, and stirring in a bit of milk and salt. Suzie dished up the chicken and some peas, and we sat down for a nice dinner with 2 glasses of Riesling.

"How far is Silver Lake?" Suzie asked.

"About eleven miles," I replied. The chicken was delicious.

"So, would it cost four times as much as the 3 miles into Barnstable Town?"

"No, because there would be no bridge to build." I scooped up some peas. Peas with butter and a little salt. Soooo good.

"And," I added. "The building ordinances for Silver County would not be as strict as Barnstable County..."

Suzie sipped some wine. She smiled, "You know, Coup has always been more closely associated with Silver Lake than Barnstable Town anyway."

Of course I knew this. We had all rattled down the dusty Route U to school in Silver Lake in the big yellow bus. That's where Suzie and I and Dwight and Emma had all formed our bonds. But eleven miles of road to pave... That had to be expensive.

Didn't it?

After we had cleared the dinner dishes and loaded the dishwasher, I said "Feel like a drive out to Indian Bend?"

"Sure," Suzie smiled. "I'll grab a sweater."

We climbed into my old truck with Suzie nestled next to me on the bench seat and rumbled down Main St., waving at a few people coming out of Holsteins. We proceeded down the hill, the same street now being Route U, and turned left onto the gravel track leading to Dwight and Emma's place, then beyond to Indian Bend, now more properly known as the "USGS Center For Antiquities Study Area."

As we neared Dwight's house we could see it was dark in the approaching twilight, but we could also see flickers of flame farther down by Silver Creek as it curved around to form Indian Bend. I proceeded slowly toward the fire, the truck bouncing along the increasingly rough road.

Dwight had a small fire started, with a ready supply of wood a short distance away. Improvised log seats were arranged around the fire pit, a leftover from the days when Indian Bend had been a marginally successful commercial campground.

"Hello Muskrats!" Dwight called as we clambered out of the truck and Suzie gave him a big hug, and a sniff. "I guess that's not coffee," she said, nodding at the aluminum cup he held. Homer levered himself up from his spot near the fire and walked stiffly to Suzy, his tail swinging in huge arcs behind him. The old hound's red and white coat was fading to a light gray, but he greeted Suzie with big licks to her scrunched-up face as she squatted to meet him.

Dwight smiled, "No coffee, but you're welcome to help yourself," he motioned toward a cooler behind a log.

I walked over, pulled out another cup, scooped some ice from the cooler and added whiskey from the open bottle of Jack Daniels. I looked at Suzie, but she shook her head.

We all three sat looking at the fire, the sky turning orange toward the west, and a deep purple to the east. Homer leaned against Suzie as she softly stroked his side.

"I wish Emma was here," Suzie said, leaning over to give Dwight a squeeze around his shoulders.

"She is," he said, touching his heart. "Right here."

We sat for a while in silence. The sky continued to darken, and in contrast the flames seemed to grow brighter. "Sometimes, when I look at the fire long enough, I imagine Emma there, laughing. Playful as ever," Dwight said softly, his eyes glistening. "She's barefoot, in a gingham dress, twirling and dancing." He shook his head. "I guess that's how I'll always remember her," he grimaced. "She never had to grow old like the rest of us, with aching bones and wrinkles."

"Not something I'm looking forward to," Suzie laughed, lightening the mood. "I'll just keep coloring my hair and applying more makeup, and you'll never see me look a day over thirty."

"Hear hear," I said, toasting with my cup and taking a drink. Dwight did the same, and Suzie held her hand out towards me. I handed her my cup and she took a healthy slug.

"Geez," she said. "Fire water at an Indian Camp?" Dwight smiled. "Isn't alcohol prohibited on a federal park area?" she asked.

"If you see a ranger coming, please let me know," Dwight said.

"And we'll destroy the evidence," I added.

We sat quietly for a bit, until Suzie reached for another drink and realized the cup was empty. She gathered the cups and refilled them. As the sky darkened into night, the moon shone on the USGS tent up the hill and behind the firepit, its white canvas reflecting a rectangle of moonlight. Farther down the hillside Silver creek tumbled over a limestone lens in a multitude of tiny waterfalls sending the sound of trickling water to echo down the valley. The original plan for the interstate would have had it crossing right through the area where we now sat, waterfalls replaced with diesel fumes.

"Suzie had an idea," I said as Dwight reached behind himself for another log, tossing it on the fire.

"Always a good sign, considering she's the brains of the outfit," teased Dwight. "What's her idea?

"What if we were to pave Highway U west to Silver Lake instead of east to Barnstable Town?" I asked.

Dwight thought. He sipped, then leaned back on the log, looking up at the sky.

We all just sat, enjoying the fire, the company, and to be honest, the whiskey. The implications of the idea were percolating through our heads.

"There are a lot of advantages to that," Dwight said at last. "The whole project would be in Silver County. There would be no bridge to build. But eleven miles is a lot of road to pave. I wonder what that would cost?"

"I have no idea," I replied. "But I bet it's cheaper than building a bridge across Silver Creek in Barnstable County."

Dwight nodded. "I'll bet you're right. And it wouldn't have the stink of the Honorable Randall Barnes attached to it."

"What do you say we run over to Silver Lake and talk to Stu Hutchins tomorrow?" I asked.

"Do you need to run this past Coup and the City Council first?" asked Suzie.

We thought about this for a bit, staring at the fire. Dwight shifted his feet and leaned forward, holding his cup with both hands. "No," he said. "This is too good of an idea to let them screw it up."

"Besides," I added. "We were instructed to explore the idea of paving a road into town without getting an exit from the interstate."

"Yeah," agreed Dwight. "We're just looking in the opposite direction."

Chapter 8

Stu Hutchins was a bear of a man, a red beard and mop of hair to match. His office was in a partitioned Quonset hut of corrugated steel, the county highway department offices of Silver County just north of Silver Lake. It was on the north and south state highway just north of its junction with Route U, which was paved through the town. Stu's office door was open, and Dwight and I walked in to find Stu leaning back in his chair, feet on an open drawer, sipping coffee with a box of doughnuts on the desk.

Stu looked up and smiled, "Howdy boys!" He pointed to the coffee maker on a cabinet in the corner. "Coffee's hot and fresh, help yourselves."

Dwight and I each selected a cup from an array of mugs and poured then doctored to our tastes. As we sat down on the seats opposite Stu's desk, he pushed the box of doughnuts towards us. We each grabbed one.

Stu was quiet while we munched and sipped. The morning air was crisp and clean, an open window letting a fresh breeze blow through the office and down the hallway, where the clanking of tools on steel and concrete echoed.

Dwight finished the last of his doughnut, licked his fingers, and washed it down with coffee. "Route U", he said. "What would it take to pave it?"

Stu reached for another doughnut, leaned back and took a bite. He stared out the window into the distance and thought. I snagged another doughnut as well.

"Machinery, men, material, and money," Stu said, then paused to work on his doughnut. He took his feet off the drawer and swiveled to face us. "For machinery, we have an old Blaw-Knox paver out back that needs a little work, and we have 2 dump trucks to transport the hot mix, but we would need at least two more, a total of six would be better. And some kind of roller."

"For manpower, Ralph, our supervisor knows how to run the paver when its running, and we have 2 other guys who could drive the trucks. So, we would need more truck drivers, someone to run the roller, signal crew of at least 2."

Stu finished his doughnut and walked to the coffee pot for a refill. "For material, we would need to spread a fresh base of gravel, that's available from the quarry 15 miles north, but for the hot mix asphalt we would have to go 30 miles south to the nearest plant."

"Tell us about the money," said Dwight.

Stu smiled as he sat back down. "That's always the kicker, isn't it?" He rearraigned himself and sipped on his coffee. "The most expensive part is the hot mix asphalt. Figure $20,000 a mile. So, for eleven miles, $220,000. Add to that the gravel base, maybe $50,000. We have an arrangement with Bond County to lend trucks to each other when needed, so we can save some money there. I think they have a roller as well."

He set his coffee down, and spread his hands, "Either of you fellas drive a truck?"

Dwight and I looked at each other, then back at Stu. "Yes," I said. "We can drive a truck."

"Well," said Stu, "Let's say we can round up a crew of my county employees and some volunteers from Coup. Limit the personnel expense to what the county is already paying us. Equipment we already have or can borrow. I'll ballpark the cost at $300,00, which is essentially the cost of materials." He sat back in his chair and sipped his coffee.

Dwight looked at me. I said, "Could we expect Silver County to put up a portion of that?"

Stu nodded. "We would have to put it before the county board, and you know how they hate to spend money, but they might go half."

Dwight grinned. I was cautiously optimistic. "If we wanted to move forward on this, what would we need to do?" I asked.

"Tell me," Stu said. "Is it true you may ask the state to skip putting an exit in for Route U?"

"Yes," I admitted, and Dwight nodded in agreement.

"The point of this paving idea is to connect Coup with the outside world," I said. "But we don't want all the traffic and change an exit would create."

"I hear ya," nodded Stu. "I am thankful the new interstate is way over by you and not here by Silver Lake." He leaned forward for emphasis, and said softly "You know, sometimes decisions and actions can have unintended consequences."

He sat back in his chair and picked up his coffee. Dwight and I looked at each other. "To get this rolling, I would need an official proposal from the city of Coup with a promise of $150,000 which I would present to the County Board," Stu motioned to us. "And y'all would be welcome to be there when I present it to show interest and answer any questions."

"And the proposal?" asked Dwight. "What should it say?"

"Nothing fancy," replied Stu. "Just a page stating your wish to have Route U paved with asphalt to county standards with a promise to pay half, and you can quote me as estimating the total cost at $300,000."

"So, all we have to do, really, is find $150,000", said Dwight, with a glance at me.

Chapter 9

"You can't be serious!" exclaimed Harold, his face twisted in incredulity.

He stood in the center of our circle in the back of Holstein's. The rest of us sat quietly, staring vaguely in the direction of the floor. Bill, as usual, maintained his vigil by the door, sipping on a tall boy.

"Pay a hundred fifty thousand dollars to pave the road to Silver Lake instead of getting a free on-ramp to a new interstate that's right in our own back yard?" Harold shook his head in disbelief. "This is insanity!" He slumped into his chair.

After a few moments of uncomfortable silence, Mayor Coup cleared his voice. "Harold has a good point." He looked around the assemblage. "Many would totally agree with him that it seems ludicrous to spend money we don't have to pay for something, namely paved access to the outside world, which is free for the asking. Moreover, many would argue that the free connection to the interstate is far better than the access gained by an improved connection to Silver Lake."

"I would also agree," the Mayor continued "That the option of connecting to Barnstable Town, though much closer, is cost prohibitive due to the cost of a bridge over Silver Creek and the unwillingness of Barnstable County to share the cost."

"So, I believe the options facing us are," he held up a finger. "One, to connect with the new interstate via a free ramp, paid for by the state." He held up a second finger, "Two, to raise one hundred fifty thousand dollars and propose to Silver County that we pave Route U to the west."

There was silence in the room.

"There is a third option," said Bill from behind me. We all turned to look.

"What?" I asked.

"Do nothing," Bill replied. "Often that's the best option. Its worked for us for years..."

Harold laughed, an involuntary laugh that led to a small choking and coughing fit.

"I'm not sure we can do 'nothing' at this point." I offered. "I think the carrot of improved outside access has been dangled in front of too many of the townsfolk for us to simply do nothing."

Dwight nodded in agreement. "I think he's right."

Ernesto sat in silence, his arms folded, his feet splayed out in front of his chair.

"Even if we did decide to pave Route U to Silver Lake," began Harold. "How would we raise the hundred and fifty thousand?" He spread his arms out, palms up. "We have no city tax. Without that, I don't see how we could pass a bond vote or take out a loan. And surely you aren't going to ask the towns people to submit to a new tax for something that could be available free…"

Again there was silence. Harold's frustration seemed to permeate the room.

"Of course, you are right," agreed Mayor Coup, in a somewhat defeated tone.

"Take up a collection," said Bill. We all looked at him.

"What?" asked Harold. "Raise a hundred fifty thousand collecting dollars and dimes?" He shook his head. "Maybe we should have a bake sale," he said with sarcasm.

"I'd be good for twenty-five thousand," said Dwight. Harold's jaw dropped.

"Me too," said Ernesto.

"Are you crazy?" asked Harold. "Where would you get that kind of money?"

"Land sales," said Bill.

I nodded. "Harold, several of us have land being taken by the new freeway. We're getting paid rather handsomely for that land."

Harold had a dazed expression.

Mayor Coup added in a calming voice, "We know you don't have any land being taken Harold, so we wouldn't expect you to be able to make a major contribution. I suppose I could also contribute twenty-five thousand towards the cause if we decided to take that approach."

"Suzie might kill me, but I'll go twenty-five as well," I said.

"She'd be more likely to kill you if you were a hold out," smiled Dwight.

"If you add in twenty-five from me, that brings us to a hundred twenty-five thousand," said Bill.

"Aw, hell," said Dwight. "If we each bump it to 30 thousand, we'd have the whole boat."

Chapter 10

"It's amazing," said Stu.

"I've never seen anything like it," agreed Randy Muniz, the County Road Team Supervisor.

Dwight and I were seated in Stu's office, a fresh box of doughnuts purchased by me open on Stu's desk. We were all munching and sipping coffee, discussing the activity in the garage behind the office.

"Normally the crew doesn't take to being ordered around," Randy expanded on his topic. "They figure they know how to do their jobs, and don't appreciate directives. They operate best if you tell them the broad outline of the job to be done, then let them do it."

Stu nodded in agreement. "But this Palmetter fellow, he's got them runnin and fetchin like I've never seen."

Randy said, "I think its because they realize he really knows what he's talking about, and they don't."

"When he rolled up in that old '53 Chevy pickup, it really got their attention," said Stu. "It's all original, unrestored, but in perfect working order. That's hard to accomplish without doing a full restoration, and it's a sign of a real mechanic."

Randy nodded. "It gave him instant street cred. They're soaking up knowledge, and he's explaining to them as they go what is happening and why they're doing each step. Right now, he's showing them how to lap the valves for the old diesel on the paver."

"Dirksen automotive, they have the contract to perform maintenance and repairs on county equipment," Randy continued, reaching for another doughnut. "They sent their best mechanic out to take a look at it, and he spent the first 15 minutes trying to figure out where to plug his diagnostic computer in."

There was general chuckling around the room. Dwight spilt some of his coffee, but I managed to set mine on the floor before I did the same."

"No computer hookup on a 1964 Blaw-Knox paver," Stu agreed. "That's when I called you and asked if Coup had anyone who could work on old equipment," he shook his head. "I had no idea y'all had someone like this Palmetter fella."

"Best thing is," said Randy, "he doesn't need a full machine shop to work. He's doing all this with power hand tools."

"When he said the engine needed a total rebuild, I figured it would set us back a month or more," Stu rose and headed for the coffee pot. "He said he would have it finished in a week, and I didn't believe him."

"You were wrong," stated Randy.

"Yup," Stu agreed. "Randy finished spreading the gravel with the grader this morning, so I think we'll be ready to start paving Monday."

"What time do you want us here?" I asked.

"Best to get an early start," said Stu. "Temperatures are warm enough to not be a problem. If we can have truck drivers here at 6 am and signal crew here by 6:30, then we can have the paver in position to start paving at 7 am when the first truckload of asphalt arrives."

"Don't want to leave the asphalt sitting in the trucks too long," said Randy, "or it'll start to harden."

"That'll be more of an issue as we get closer to Coup," said Stu, "because we'll have an extra ten miles to transport. But by that time we'll have the operation running pretty smooth."

Randy nodded in agreement. We were out of doughnuts, so Dwight and I thanked them and left.

Chapter 11

I pulled my assigned dump truck to the right, leaving plenty of room behind me as Dwight fed the load of his assigned dump truck into the paving machine, waves of heat rising as the noisy contraption inched forward, gently pushing Dwight's idling truck ahead of it.

To my left Harry Palmetter's black 1953 Chevrolet Advance Design pickup passed by with its large "Follow Me" sign in black over yellow, topped by flashing lights mounted behind the cab. A string of traffic followed him until he reached Mary Palmetter, her hair under a bandanna topped by a white hard hat, an orange vest around her shoulders. She waited while Harry spun the old truck around, then aimed it back toward Silver Lake, preparing to lead the westbound traffic which had accumulated behind Mary's hand-held STOP sign.

"Leading traffic westbound," came Harry's voice over the radio mounted in my truck's cab.

"Ten-four, eastbound stopped," came the reply from Mrs. Hutchens, Stu's wife stationed a mile to the west.

The speaker crackled, then Stu's voice came on. "Dwight, that'll be your last load for the day. And after Sam drops his, can y'all come over and chat with me for a bit?"

"Yes, Sir," replied Dwight. I echoed the same.

Since we had just entered the town of Coup itself, one lane of newly paved road stretching behind us, I parked the big dump truck in the parking lot behind Holstein's, joined the waiting Dwight and walked over to where Stu was leaning against a fence post watching the paver laying the last load of asphalt for the day being emptied from a truck driven by one of his regular drivers into the paver.

"I've been doing some calculating," said Stu. "Tomorrow we'll be at the approach to the bridge, then we can turn around and start paving the other lane back towards Silver Lake."

"Sounds good," I said, with Dwight nodding in agreement.

"Only thing is," said Stu, "We're halfway done and we haven't used nearly half of the asphalt I ordered as part of the contract with the asphalt provider."

He paused to let this sink in.

"So, what do we do?" asked Dwight. "Widen the other lane going back, or get a refund on the contract?"

"Can't get a refund," Stu replied. "And we're already at the maximum lane width on this old paver."

We stood in silence, the roller crowding the heels of the paving machine as it jolted forward leaving the last of its fresh pavement ready to be compacted by the roller. The waves of heat wafting up from the asphalt brought the strong smell of hot oil, not an unpleasant odor to me.

"I don't know," said Dwight, thoughtfully. "Is there anything else we can do with the asphalt?"

"Asphalt ain't good for nothin' but paving," replied Stu.

"How about the city streets here in Coup?" I asked. "Could we pave them?"

"We'd have to put down a gravel base first for drainage," replied Stu. "But I think we could probably do that."

"Hell, we got all the equipment right here," said Dwight.

"And asphalt to spare," I added.

Stu nodded. "Okay, we'll finish the eastbound lane tomorrow, then switch to the city streets. In the morning I'll divert 2 of the boys to start spreading gravel so we should be set. I figure about a day and a half should do it, then we'll start paving the westbound lane back toward Silver Lake."

Dwight and I both nodded, and as we started to leave I held out my hand to Stu. "Thank you," I said as he shook it. Dwight followed my lead and did the same.

As we crossed over the street to Holsteins where we had parked our pickups that morning, Dwight was grinning from ear to ear. "Holy crap," he said just loud enough for me to hear. "Ain't no way he overestimated that much. He planned to pave our city streets all along – he just waited until we – you, suggested it."

I smiled and nodded in agreement. "He probably couldn't suggest using county resources to pave our city streets. That idea had to come from us."

"Son-of-a-bitch," Dwight said as we got to our trucks. "Man, what a difference that'll make. The townspeople are gonna love that."

"We owe him big time," I agreed.

Dwight leaned against the bed of my pickup. "Did you see that Hildebrand won the primary?"

"Yup," I replied. "He'll be challenging the Governor this fall."

"You know," said Dwight. "He and Barney go way back to when they both ran for the state house."

"I remember," I said. "It got pretty rough for a local election."

"Should be interesting to see how Hildebrand gets along against the Governor."

"You can bet he won't be getting any help from Barnstable County."

"Makes me like him all the more," smiled Dwight.

Chapter 12

The old wrap-around verandah at Holstein's had been granted a new life. It had been power washed and re-stained, with wrought iron mesh metal tables and chairs placed under its awnings. A new waitress had joined Candy and was taking orders from the assembled group.

Always a place where town folk could join an existing table or sit by themselves as they chose, two tables had been joined together overlooking the newly completed paved Route U. Suzie and I were seated with Dwight and Bill Belmont, and Harry and Mary Palmetter had just joined us.

Harry and Mary ordered iced tea, and Bill tilted his tall boy to indicate he was ready for another. The waitress, Rochelle, sister of Suzie's part time stylist Chloe, headed in to fetch the drinks.

"I got a call from the Silver County School Superintendent," said Harry. "Offered me a job teaching engine repair for the high school."

"Well, I think you'd be great at that," I said.

Mary nodded. "That's what I told him. He needs something to do."

Harry looked down at the table. "Thing is, that seems too restrictive to me." He looked over at Mary and smiled. "You know I don't like limits on what I can work on or what I can do when I'm working. A school shop situation – I would be limited to showing kids how to start a project, then a bell would ring and everybody vamooses!" He shook his head. "I don't think I could just stop like that."

"Open a trade school," said Bill as a new tall boy was set in front of him.

We all looked at Bill.

"There's the old feed store across the street," he said. "Clean it up, put in a lift and a few tools. See if the high school would offer half-day classes."

"Don't limit it to engine repair," suggested Dwight. "Do full restorations. There's nobody teaching that stuff anymore – it's a dying art."

"You could even offer continuing education for post-graduates," added Suzie.

"You've still got all your old equipment from your old shop stored in the sheds," prodded Mary. "I'll bet you could set up a shop pretty easily."

Harry sipped his Iced tea. We all sat quietly.

Ernesto's black Escalade purred to a stop in front of Holstein's and he emerged. "Management's gonna have to pave this parking lot," he smiled as he took off his wide brimmed black hat. "Everything else in this town is paved, but my Escalade gets dusty pulling into the lot!"

Mary pulled out the empty chair next to her. "Ernesto," she said. "Won't you please join us?"

"Thank you, Mary," he said and sat, placing his hat on a bench behind him.

Rochelle appeared refilling tea, and I motioned to my beer and Suzie's wine.

"Tea for me please, Rochelle," said Ernesto.

"Sure, Uncle Ernesto," Rochelle smiled and turned to go back inside.

"Are you two related?" asked Mary.

"Not really," replied Ernesto. "It's more an honorary title."

Mary looked at him questioningly.

"Well," Ernesto began. "Her and Chloe's father worked for me for years and wanted to become a citizen. I helped him and after he was successful, he brought his girlfriend from Mexico and sponsored her to get her citizenship. So, when Rochelle and Chole were born, they were both full U. S. citizens from birth."

"That's beautiful," said Mary.

"And they've stayed close ever since," added Suzie. "Chloe works for me on Saturdays, and she's a delight."

Rochelle brought drinks and everyone settled in.

"I just came from Barnstable," said Ernesto.

Everyone looked at him.

"You know, I sit in on the political party meetings," he smiled. "Since my property extends into Barnstable County they welcome me."

"I thought you were connected," I said.

"Well," smiled Ernesto. "I don't know about 'connected', but I can tell you that Barney is worried."

"You mean Mayor Barnes?" asked Mary. "Why would he be worried?"

"I think the polls have them scared," said Ernesto. "Hildebrand is running strong, and the governor is not looking that good for re-election. That's one of the reasons he pushed ahead on this new Interstate highway – trying to curry favor in this part of the state."

"But why would the Governor's race impact Mayor Barnes?" asked Mary.

"Barnstable Town and County have been some of the current Governor's strongest supporters. And Hildebrand and Mayor Barnes hate each other."

"So, if the Governor loses re-election," said Suzie. "Mayor Barnes will have to deal with Hildebrand as Governor."

"Exactly," nodded Ernesto. "So, Barney pulled me aside at the meeting and asked if I could let my workers have election day off so they could vote."

"Ah," said a chorus of voices around the table.

"But, if they aren't citizens they can't vote," said Mary.

"Mayor Barnes hinted that the polls in Barnstable won't be checking ID's too closely. They'll be taking them as 'provisional' ballots," said Ernesto.

"Are you going to do it?" asked Mary.

"I may give them the day off work," said Ernesto. "But I don't think any of them are really interested in the election."

Chapter 13

Bill and I could see Dwight walking toward us as we stood on the verandah at Holstein's. Dwight was wearing a lined denim jacket and his ever-present straw cowboy hat even in the stiff northerly breeze.

We had been speculating how, or whether, Dwight would arrive. The construction of the overpass for Route U had caused a temporary closure necessitating a detour of over 50 miles through Barnstable town, then north to Forrest City, west to a state highway, then south to Silver Lake, and back east on the now-paved Route U to Coup. Dwight had done the sensible thing and walked the mile and a half through the construction area where grading of the new interstate was in progress.

"Short notice meeting," said Dwight as he climbed the steps, no need to stomp his feet at the top now that Holstein's lot was newly paved.

"The new governor doesn't want to waste any time handing out good news," replied Bill.

"You think it's gonna be good news?" I asked as we turned to go inside.

"Depends on who you are I suspect," said Dwight.

As we walked through the bar to get to the meeting hall, Bill waggled his now empty beer can towards Candy, who smiled and nodded. We proceeded into the room where Rellette and Thomas had already set up their easel, although this time they were joined by a very fit middle-aged black man dressed in a sport coat over a golf shirt. He, like Thomas, was seated on one side of Rellette, who stood by the easel.

Coup was already seated as was Ernesto. Even Harold was already in place since Bill and I had dawdled awaiting Dwight's arrival. Bill assumed his customary perch, tilted against the wall while Dwight and I joined the seated semi-circle.

Coup nodded at Rellette. "We are all now present, you may begin when you like."

Rellette hesitated. "We were expecting we might be joined by representatives from Barnstable county and city governments," he looked over at Thomas. Thomas looked at the black man.

"Let's go ahead," he said. "We can schedule another meeting for Barnstable next week."

"They're probably affected by the construction closures," suggested Thomas.

The black man nodded. "No telling when or if they'll show up here."

Rellette nodded and cleared his throat. "Welcome, everyone, and thank you for letting us give this update on such short notice." He motioned to his right, "You all remember Mr. Thomas, and this is Mr. Carl Samuels, the new Secretary of Transportation."

"Welcome, Mr. Secretary," said Coup, rising and extending his hand.

Samuels also rose and shook hands with Coup, then proceeded around the circle as we all stood and offered our hands. Even Bill walked up and shook hands with the Secretary.

"Thank you," said Samuels. Then to Rellette, "Go ahead Monte."

"Thank you, Mr. Secretary," replied Rellette.

Turning to his easel, he pulled back the cover sheet to reveal a revised map of the area.

"The new governor has declared that the runaway costs surrounding the interstate expansion project must be curtailed." He pointed at the Route U overpass. "We realize that the city of Coup had requested to forgo an exit for County Route U, but cost overruns on the revision of the former federal highway through Barnstable Town has caused us to re-evaluate that decision."

"So, we're getting an exit for Route U after all?" asked Ernesto.

"Well, yes," nodded Rellette. "The paved connection to the county seat in Silver Lake is very attractive." He pointed to the map with his laser. "This also allows us to eliminate the..."

A commotion at the back of the room caused him to pause. We all turned to look, and saw The Honorable Mayor Randall Barnes followed by Barnstable County Commissioner Wilton Greenville enter the room. Both appeared harried and out of breath, with Barney's face a disconcerting shade of red.

"What the hell is this?" demanded Barney.

"It's a meeting of the Coup City Council'" replied Coup, standing to face the intruders.

"Hell, I know that," steamed Barney. "I mean why have the meeting in this God forsaken backwater rather than in Barnstable?" He turned to Ernesto. "And you!" He shook his head in disgust. "I might have known you were a traitor, here in the damned City Council. Why would a wide spot in the road even need a council?"

"Please calm down Mayor Barnes," said Coup in a steady, even tone. "If you wish to remain here, I insist you maintain decorum."

Barney wheeled to face him. "I'm just here to find out what kind of tricks the new governor is up to." He peered up at Coup, who was a good head taller, and Barney managed to tilt his head back far enough that he was looking down his nose as he did so. "You can just stay out of it, old man."

Coup stepped closer to Barney, and still maintaining his even tone said "You will refer to me as Mayor Coup in these proceedings. Now sit down," he pointed to two chairs that Bill had pulled up to join the gallery. Greenville, who had remained silent, pulled the still fuming Barney by the shoulder and got him seated.

Rellette composed himself and returned to his easel. "As I was saying, the governor has tasked us with reducing the out of control costs associated with the state's portion of the new interstate highway construction." He pointed to the US Highway running north to south through Barnstable.

"In particular, the crowding of businesses along the former US Highway corridor makes the widening and improvements necessary for a business loop prohibitively expensive. To eliminate that expense, we have chosen to redesignate that highway as a secondary state route and eliminate the exits to the north and south of Barnstable town."

"You can't do that!" Barney was up and out of his seat. "The plans for the Interstate Business Loop have been in place for years!"

Thomas was now on his feet and motioned to Rellette with his palm down.

"Yes," Thomas nodded. "But that advance knowledge has allowed land speculators to purchase parcels along the route and encroach upon the right of way needed to widen the street to accommodate the increased traffic load. This has caused the budget of the project to explode with overruns." He looked specifically at Barney and continued, "As stewards of the interests for residents of Barnstable you should have kept a watchful eye to prevent this situation. Standard practice in most communities is to place a moratorium for improvements on any corridor-adjacent landholdings. It would appear that Barnstable County and Barnstable Town have neglected to do so to their detriment."

"Why would the State even care?" whined Barney. "It's a federal highway!"

"Not anymore," said Thomas calmly. "As Monte, Mr. Rellette, stated - it's a *former* US Highway. One of the advantages to the Feds in building an interstate highway is they get to turn over responsibility and maintenance of the US Highways the interstate replaces to the state." He smiled, "And in this case the state has determined its appropriate to redesignate the highway as a secondary route."

"But you can't eliminate the exits!" exclaimed Barney. "We are the county seat for Christ's sake!"

Rellette had handed the pointer to Thomas who now aimed it at the interchange with Route U. "Both Silver County and Barnstable county seats will be accessed by the new exit for Route U," he said.

"Hell, that's just a low water bridge over Silver Creek," said Barney. "You can't expect us to use that for interstate access."

Carl Samuels stood up and cleared his throat. "Pardon me, Mr. Mayor. Mayor Barnes, am I correct?" He held out his hand.

Ignoring the hand, Barney said "And who the hell are you?"

"May I present State Secretary of Transportation Carl Samuels," said Coup, standing and extending his arm towards Samuels.

Barney turned even redder than he had been before and when he turned to shake the Secretary's hand, he found it no longer extended.

"The fact that you have only a low water bridge over county route U does reflect rather poorly on Barnstable County's management of funds," said Samuels. "Do I understand correctly that members of this community approached you some time ago and offered to share the cost of upgrading the road into Barnstable?"

"Yes," sputtered Barney. "But that wasn't their call!"

"Correct," nodded Samuels. "Yet you flatly rejected a proposal for money from outside your county to aid in improvements to your infrastructure."

"They were wanting that to help themselves," said Barney with exasperation.

"When you're dealing with outside money for improvements to your county, you shouldn't question motives too closely," said Samuels philosophically. "Money is money."

"How about the state?" Barney pointed at Rellette and Thomas. "If there's improvements needed to connect with the Interstate, shouldn't you guys be improving Route U?"

"Route U is a county road, both in Silver County and in Barnstable County," said Samuels. "Silver County improved Route U all the way to Silver Lake and never asked the State for a dime. That's the kind of community stewardship and responsibility that impresses Governor Hildebrand."

"Mr. Secretary," Greenville had finally found his voice. "With only the low water bridge connecting Barnstable County to the rest of the state, it would unfairly isolate the citizens of Barnstable County."

"Barnstable will still have the former US highway, now a state highway, connecting to Forrest City in the north and points south. The state will continue to maintain the highway. Residents can access the interstate at Forrest City or at the next exit south, which is what, Monte – 20 miles?"

Rellette nodded, "Closer to 23 miles, Mr. Secretary."

Samuels smiled, "So there, Mr. Greenville. Residents of Barnstable County not only have access to the interstate through the Route U low water bridge, they also have access through Forrest City and farther south. They just won't have the traffic generated by exits immediately north and south creating a business loop."

Barney looked dazed.

Greenville said "Barnstable County doesn't have the funds necessary to construct a proper bridge to the Route U interchange. That would ruin the county!"

Samuels smiled. "Sure, there's money. In this past election season Barnstable County contributed over half a million dollars to just one single candidate. That clearly demonstrates the availability of community funds."

"Hildebrand is just upset that the money didn't go to him," exploded Barney.

"Governor Hildebrand is pleased he won the popular support of residents throughout the state in spite of a few pockets of special interests trying to keep the status quo," said Samuels. "His message of fiscal responsibility resonated with the voters, and he intends to follow through, starting with reigning in the state's portion of the expenditures associated with this new interstate."

"This will ruin Me – I mean, Barnstable Town," cried Barney, almost in tears.

Greenville took him by the arm and helped him toward the door at the back of the room. Barney shuffled along, still in a daze as they passed through the door.

The boys from the state wrapped up their presentation and shook hands around the Coup council contingent, took their easel and left.

The air was quiet as we all sat, the only sound that of a Coors tall boy being drained by Bill at the back of the room.

"Encroachment on right of way," said Bill. "Only one person I know would be stupid and arrogant enough to try that."

At length Dwight said, "Why didn't we ask the state for money to pave Route U?"

"Didn't think of it," I replied dumbly.

"All that effort and expense to prevent having an exit from the interstate to Route U in order to maintain our starry sky, and still we got an exit," Dwight shook his head.

"Stu Hutchins did mention unexpected consequences," I offered. "Maybe he saw this coming."

"He's usually a couple steps ahead of us," agreed Dwight.

Ernesto, normally quiet, cleared his throat. "I have an idea..."

Chapter 14

It was springtime again. Suzie and I were back in our swing, swaying beneath a starry sky, her head on my shoulder, but this time with a sweater wrapped around her. The grasshoppers and crickets drowned out the distant hum of traffic proceeding down the valley. The air was cool, but crisp and clear. We were, as usual, in heaven.

A lot had happened since the preceding fall. The new interstate had been completed. Another skeleton had been discovered at the USGS Center for Antiquities Study Area at Indian Bend, and Chloe had increased her hours at Suzie's salon to 3 days a week.

And, development had begun as a result of the new exit for Route U.

We heard footsteps behind us, and turned enough to see Bill approaching. "Evening, Miss Suzie," he said tilting up his cowboy hat. "May I borrow Sam for a spell?"

"Sure, Bill," smiled Suzie. "What's up?"

"I think its time we had a little Pow-Wow down at Indian Bend," said Bill. "Sam can tell you all about it."

Mystified, I arose and kissed Suzie on the top of her head. "Back in a bit," I said.

"Thank you, Miss Suzie," said Bill, and we headed toward the front of the house. As we rounded the house, I could see Ernesto's shiny black Escalade pickup idling on the street. Bill motioned me to get in front and he climbed in behind me.

Ernesto grinned a toothy grin and dropped the Escalade into drive, and we purred away. "What's the plan?" I asked.

Ernesto just pointed his thumb toward Bill in the back seat. "I'm guessing you know as much as I do."

We reached Main street, now of course the paved Route U, and turned right. We passed the old feed store with its new sign "Coup de Ville" and underneath that in smaller letters, "Classic Car Maintenance and Repair, Restorations as Needed." In a large sparkling window was parked a beautiful 1961 Cadillac Series 60 sedan in a cream yellow with a matching interior. Soft lighting allowed it to simply glow. Even the signage outside had soft downward facing lights. Not lit were smaller letters, "Vocational-Technical and Adult Education Classes" and "Harry Palmetter, Instructor."

We continued past the new gas station and mini mart which now sat on the site where Marjorie's house had once stood. The lighting theme continued; low wattage soft lights lit the parking lot, fuel pumps, and storefront, with no light allowed to reflect up into the sky. Even the concrete and paving were done with a rough non-reflective surface.

All this had been Ernesto's 'Idea'. We, the city council, had legislated requirements limiting the number of lights per square foot as well as the wattage of those lights. Overhead checks made sure no light escaped upward to contribute to the town's almost non-existent light pollution. Ernesto's brilliant idea had been turned into practical success.

The Escalade effortlessly climbed the bridge approach and passed over the newly completed Interstate highway, cars and trucks passing below us. On the far side as Route U began to go deeper into the valley, Ernesto turned left onto the gravel road leading to Dwight's place and beyond to Indian Bend.

Proceeding at a slow pace to protect his truck, we could see a glimmer of firelight down near Silver Creek. We rolled on down the hill and parked just outside the ring of firelight. As we climbed out of the truck Ernesto went around back and reached into the truck bed, flipped open a box, and pulled out a bottle and four tin cups. He carried them as we approached the fire being tended by Dwight.

"Howdy boys," he welcomed us. "Pull up a log and enjoy the fire."

Homer was lying a respectful distance from the fire, but close enough to enjoy the warmth. He lifted his head enough to take us in, then lay it back down with a few welcoming thumps of his tail on the grass.

Ernesto handed Dwight a cup, and then filled it from the bottle. He repeated the process with Bill and I, then filled one for himself. Dwight raised his cup in a toast and took a sip, pausing afterwards to smack his lips. "Good stuff," he said. "What is it?"

"Old Monroe," replied Ernesto. "Comes from a little town in Illinois outside St. Louis. Family farm grows all the ingredients and uses water from a spring on the property."

"It *is* good," I remarked. "Where do you get it?"

"Whenever I'm around St. Louis I buy a case, right there at the distillery, Stumpys. That way I always have plenty for special occasions."

"Special occasions?" I asked.

"Yeah, like when I'm drinking whiskey," smiled Ernesto.

Dwight chuckled.

We sat by the firelight and relaxed, sipping the whiskey, getting nice and toasty from the inside and the outside. The creek splashed over the little waterfalls of the riffle just below us, and the Milky Way splashed across the sky. Crickets chirped, and in the distance a low hum of traffic on the highway could be heard.

Finally, Bill said softly, "Okay Dwight, its time."

Dwight looked over at him. "Time for what?"

Bill was silent for a long moment. "The story." He took a drink of his whiskey and swallowed with a sigh. "You can tell it now. What are they gonna do, move the highway?"

Dwight was silent for a very long time. He stirred the fire with a stick and several sparks flew up into the air. He looked around at Ernesto, Bill, and Me, then nodded. "It'll be good to get this out. I've been carrying it around for a long time."

Ernesto got up and circled the group, refilling cups. Dwight reached behind him and grabbed another log while Homer arose and stretched, then slowly moved towards the Escalade with his tail wagging. Dwight positioned the log on the fire and adjusted it with his stick until he was satisfied. "Where should I start?" he asked.

"From the beginning," replied Bill. "We're in no hurry."

Dwight sighed. "You know, this property is where I grew up. In that house up on the hillside," he motioned with his head. "When Emma and I got married we moved to Memphis for a spell, then when Dad passed, we moved back here to the farm. We raised our kids here, and we all swam in Silver Creek, right down there." He motioned with his head again, then took a long pull from his cup.

"For Emma and me, this was a special place. We would build a fire right here, and speculate that Indians might have enjoyed this same spot in the same way for centuries." He paused, remembering.

"Then two things happened, at about the same time, more or less," Dwight shook his head. "First, Emma started feeling poorly, and Doctor Peters sent her to Memphis to have tests done. Then the other was the announcement of the plan to build a freeway right through this valley, crossing the creek right here."

We all sat quietly, listening, with our heads bowed while the fire crackled.

"You all know, the tests came back saying it was cancer. They recommended chemo-therapy, and Emma tried it twice, but she said it was worse than dying of cancer, so she gave it up and decided to enjoy the time she had left as best we could. We came up with a plan to stop the highway, and that really did help her spirits. We donated the land for the Signal Hill Wildlife Refuge figuring that would cause the highway to be re-routed to the west."

"But that didn't work," I said quietly.

"No, it didn't," said Dwight. "They accepted the land, then said it would have to be split into two parcels, east and west, because of the pre-existing plan for the interstate highway."

"Government assholes," said Bill.

"Damn right," agreed Dwight, and raised his cup. We all followed suit, and took hefty drinks.

Ernesto started around with the bottle again, but ran out before he got to me. "Hang on." he said, and trotted toward the truck. We heard him mumbling softly, then he rattled around in the bed and came back with a fresh bottle.

"Thank God," I said. "I was afraid I would have to go thirsty."

"No chance of that," said Ernesto, pouring. "I still have most of a case in the truck."

"Alright, Dwight," I said. "Now you can really take your time.

Dwight smiled. "It is good to get this out." He leaned back and looked up at the stars. "And Ernesto, I am so thankful for your idea to restrict lighting. That is a Godsend."

We all raised our cups and said "Hear, hear."

Dwight leaned forward and resumed his tale. "So, on Emma's deathbed, she asked me to make sure the highway would not come through our little slice of paradise here. I promised her I would never let that happen. She died not knowing whether I would be successful." Dwight paused, and stared into the fire.

"As well as she knew you, she had to know you would find a way," I said.

Dwight nodded. "I hope you're right Sam."

Bill leaned over towards Ernesto, extending his cup, and Ernesto topped him off.

Dwight continued. "I finally got smart and did some research about what *would* stop a planned highway from being constructed. It turns out there isn't much. Primarily its either an 'Endangered Species' or a 'Culturally Significant Site'.

"Ain't no endangered species hereabouts," commented Bill.

"No sir," agreed Dwight. "So Culturally Significant it had to be."

"I started auditing archaeology courses at the college until I found a senior professor I could work with. I started plying him with liquor in the evenings after classes and commiserating about how poorly he was compensated for his work. He confessed he had promised his wife he would take her to Europe, and I knew I had him. I told him of my problem, and of the promise I had made to Emma, and suggested how we could help each other out.

"He had been working on a dig in Utah and was responsible for the cataloguing of the bones found in a mass gravesite. It was easy for him to set aside some skeletons for shipment to a separate research center. He brought them here, and buried them along the hillside up there," Dwight nodded toward the USGS site up the hill.

"Then what happened?" I asked.

"He took his wife on a luxury trip to Europe at my expense, then came home and died," Dwight shook his head ruefully.

· "Son of a bitch," said Bill, with feeling.

"Yeah," agreed Dwight. "So, what was I to do? The professor had said we should wait for the ground to settle around the skeletons so they would not appear to be freshly planted, but he didn't say how long that would take. Part of the plan had been for him to discover them and supervise the dig to expose them."

"And the state didn't seem to be in a hurry to build the highway," I commented.

"Good thing," said Dwight. "So, after a few years I opened Indian Bend Campground. I focused on Boy Scout groups and kept challenging them to find Indian bones. They thought I was kidding.

"Finally, I started inviting Girl Scouts to camp here too. They were more receptive to looking for the Indian bones, and danged if the third group of campers didn't actually find them. I went back to the university and had them come examine them. I was afraid they would detect that the ground had been disturbed, but I guess my guy had been careful and thorough and they didn't raise an eyebrow. Eventually they did start to notice similarities to the bones found in Utah, and started making theories about migrations."

"So, you messed up Archeology and Anthropology for both areas," said Bill.

"I'm afraid so," smiled Dwight sheepishly.

"Well, it was for a good cause," I offered.

"Damn straight," said Dwight. "This is sacred ground. Not because of the Indian bones, but because I spread Emma's ashes all over this hillside."

"There probably *are* authentic Indian bones all over," said Ernesto. "They just haven't been found."

Dwight nodded. "Good thing the plan came together when it did, because it wasn't long afterwards the state finally got going on the highway. You fellas know the rest."

The firelight flickered across our faces as we stared and contemplated how these simple events had culminated in the situation that had finally developed.

"You know," I said. "The entire question of whether to have an exit and the development it would have caused was somewhat independent of which route the interstate took around the wildlife refuge. We would have faced the same issues even if the highway had come through here."

There were nods around the fire, and it was again quiet. Then Dwight turned to Bill and asked, "How did you know?"

"Indian bones just happened to be found in the path of a new interstate, right between 2 sections of land you had donated for a wildlife reserve. That had me suspicious to begin with," Bill replied. "Then you said you were losing a hundred large because they had rerouted the interstate to take up less of your land, all because of a half dozen Indian skeletons."

Dwight nodded in understanding.

"They had only found five skeletons," I said, slowly catching up.

"Yup," said Bill. "I thought maybe he was just generalizing, but then they found a sixth skeleton."

"I knew there were six because I had paid for six," acknowledged Dwight.

"So, the whole endeavor cost you a lot more than the hundred thousand you lost in land sales," I said.

Dwight chuckled and nodded. "I don't even want to try to tally it all up, but it was worth it," he looked around at the scene overlooking the creek. "Well worth it."

Ernesto arose and circled the group refilling cups, then sat back down and said, "I have a bit of a confession as well."

We all looked at him.

"I knew something about this, but not the whole story. Apparently, this professor needed help in planting the skeletons, and he was able to get in touch with one of my foremen who knew how to operate heavy equipment. No need to mention his name, but he came to me asking for advice. Once I found out he was being asked to help do some quiet excavation work here, I knew Dwight had a plan of some sort. I told my man to go ahead, but not to talk to anyone else about it."

"So, after the bones were found and the USGS Study Area was established, I figured it was time to move the project along. I mentioned to one of the previous governor's aids that the people in this part of the state felt pretty left out, and they would look fondly on a governor who revitalized the plan to construct the interstate."

"Son of a bitch," Dwight sat in awe.

Ernesto nodded. "I figured it was best to get it done now before the site got old and interest faded."

"Strike while the iron is hot," commented Bill.

"Well, it all worked," I offered.

There were nods around the fire, and we were again quiet. Dwight turned to get another log, and there was a figure stepping into the firelight.

"I am so proud of you boys," said Suzie, wrapped in a blanket, bending down to give Dwight a hug, Homer at her side.

"Thank you," said Dwight.

"And I know Emma is proud of you too," she gave him another hug, then walked over and sat next to me, taking the cup from my hand. Homer sat next to her and placed his head on her thigh.

I put my arm around her. "How did you get here?" I asked.

"I walked, silly," she replied and took a sip from the cup.

"Well, where'd you get the blanket?"

"Ernesto hooked me up," she said with a wink, drained my cup, and placed her head on my shoulder.

A log on the fire suddenly popped, sending sparks swirling into the sky to join the billions of stars shining down from the heavens, where a sharp eye could have noticed a pretty girl gayly twirling in a gingham dress...

For more information about lessening the impact of light pollution, please visit:

International Dark-Sky Association at **darksky.org**